Be Brave,
Morgan!

Morgan
the Brave

Morgan the

by Ted Staunton
and Will Staunton

illustrated by Bill Slavin

Brave

Formac Publishing Company Limited
Halifax

Text copyright © 2017 by Ted Staunton and Will Staunton
Illustrations copyright © 2017 by Bill Slavin
Published in Canada in 2017. Published in the United States in 2018.

Formac Publishing Company Limited recognizes the support of the Province of
Nova Scotia through the Department of Communities, Culture and Heritage.
We are pleased to work in partnership with the Province of Nova Scotia
to develop and promote our cultural resources for all Nova Scotians. We
acknowledge the support of the Canada Council for the Arts, which last year
invested $153 million to bring the arts to Canadians throughout the country.
This project has been made possible in part by the Government of Canada.

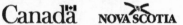

Cover design: Tyler Cleroux
Cover image: Bill Slavin

Library and Archives Canada Cataloguing in Publication

Staunton, Ted, 1956-, author
        Morgan the brave / by Ted Staunton and Will
Staunton ; illustrated by Bill Slavin.

(Be brave, Morgan!)
ISBN 978-1-4595-0497-4 (hardcover)

        I. Slavin, Bill, illustrator II. Staunton, Will, author
III. Title. IV. Series: Staunton, Ted, 1956- . Be brave, Morgan!)

PS8587.T334M6723 2017   jC813'.54   C2017-903293-3

Published by: Distributed in Canada by: Distributed in the US by:
Formac Publishing   Formac Lorimer Books   Lerner Publisher Services
Company Limited   5502 Atlantic Street   1251 Washington Ave. N.
5502 Atlantic Street   Halifax, NS, Canada   Minneapolis, MN, USA
Halifax, Nova Scotia,   B3H 1G4   55401
Canada, B3H 1G4   www.lernerbooks.com
www.formac.ca

Printed and bound in Canada.

Manufactured by Friesens Corporation in Altona, Manitoba,
Canada in August 2017.

Job #236681

Contents

1 The Invitation   7

2 Stuck   15

3 Excuses, Excuses   23

4 It Can't be that Bad . . . Right?   33

5 Revenge!   43

6 Chilling Tales   51

7 A Cunning Plan   61

8 Disaster!   69

9 Desperate Measures   77

10 Escape!   87

Chapter One

The Invitation

"BOO!" A scarecrow with witchy hair zaps out around the corner of the school.

"**GAAH!**" I jump back, dropping my cookies on the ground. Aldeen Hummel grabs them before I can. It's the third time she's zapped me this week.

"Hey!" I say, **"Those are mine."**

"Scaredy-cat tax," she says, cramming one in her mouth. I don't complain. Complaining gets you a killer noogie. Aldeen is not just a scarecrow, she is the Godzilla of grade three. She shoves the other cookie back at me. Before I can take it, someone calls, "Kiss and make up!"

It's Curtis. Aldeen's eyes squinch up behind her glasses. Curtis joined our class a couple of months ago.

Today he's wearing red and white sunglasses and a matching striped jacket.

With his hair gelled up he looks like a giant birthday candle.

"Cool, huh?" he says. "My dad got this stuff for me in L.A."

He hands me an envelope. "My birthday's on Saturday.

Party at my place, everyone's coming." He hands an envelope to Aldeen. "My parents said I have to invite you, too."

Aldeen's face gets redder than Curtis's jacket. Her lips bunch up. Curtis just keeps talking.

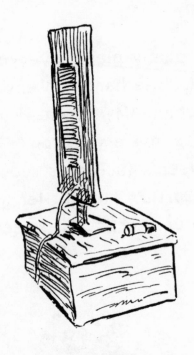

"Not only do I have the most awesome backyard for parties in the world, we're going to watch *Brain Eater*, the scariest movie ever. My parents don't even know I have it, so don't squeal."

"Awesome," I say. "I love scary movies."

Curtis is already jogging off to the other kids. "Bring a good present," he calls over his shoulder.

I turn to Aldeen.

She's gone, to give Steffi a noogie.

She's taken my cookie and left me with a problem.

Chapter Two

Stuck

The problem is not my kidnapped cookie. The problem is, I do not love scary movies.

I hate scary movies. They scare me.

What could be in the scariest movie ever made?

Mummies?

Vampires? **Aliens?**

Alien-vampire -mummies?

I get creeped out just thinking about it.

Everyone whispers about it all afternoon. Nobody's seen *Brain Eater*, but everybody seems to know something about it.

"I heard they use real earwax," whispers Charlie.

"My brother watched it," says Matt, "and he passed out!"

Melissa hisses, "Did you hear what they make the spaghetti out of?"

I feel worse and worse. Even Aldeen's witchy hair gives me an extra chill. I don't want to know about the spaghetti, or the earwax. I don't want to pass out.

Dad's in the kitchen when I get home from school. I grab a couple of cookies so I'll be too full to eat the mushrooms he's washing for dinner.

"How was school, kiddo?" asks Dad.

I say, "Curtis invited me to his birthday party on Saturday, but I don't want to go."

"Why not?"

Dad chops the mushrooms. Don't brains look all pale like that?

"I just don't like Curtis very much." This is true. Besides, if I tell him about the movie, Dad will call Curtis's parents. Then I'll get blamed for being the chicken that tattled and wrecked the party.

Dad rinses a tomato. "He's still pretty new to your class, Morgan. It can be tough making friends. Who else is invited?"

"The whole class," I say.

Dad smiles. "Then there will be lots of kids to have fun with. You can play with Charlie."

He chops again. Tomato guts ooze onto the cutting board. I gulp and back away.

"Gonna like dinner," he calls after me. "Your favourite. Spaghetti!"

Chapter Three

Excuses, Excuses

Next morning, Mark tells
Curtis he can't come to the
party because he's going to a
basketball game. "Yeah, right,"
Curtis scoffs. "You're just
chicken because of *Brain Eater*.
Mark's a chicken, bwak buck buck!"

Everyone laughs. I give up
my plan to tell Curtis I have to
go mountain climbing.

I don't like this one bit. Curtis
and Aldeen both have me

scared
of being
scared.

I don't know what to do
about Curtis, but I know what
to do about Aldeen. I think
all through Math about it. At
recess I'll go out the opposite

way and scare her. She'll be
peeking around the corner,
waiting for me. I'll tiptoe up,
ninja-ghost quiet behind her,
lean in, and — "Boo!" I yell
right in class, and jerk awake
from my daydream. Curtis
squawks and topples off his

chair. Everyone laughs again, except our teacher, Mrs. Ross. "Morgan!" She frowns. "Save it for recess. And Curtis, don't lean your chair so far back."

Curtis gets back up.

"You wanna get dumped from my party?"

he hisses at me.

Part of me thinks *Oh, yes.* The rest of me is scared of getting left out. "Sorry," I mumble.

After school, Aldeen comes over like she does sometimes,

until her grandma can pick her
up. Mom says it's too nice to
be inside, and gives us carrots
for a snack. "Use the new
croquet set," she says, and
sends us to the backyard.

I groan, but really croquet is
my kind of sport: no running,
no tackling and you can eat
while you play. All you do is hit
your ball with a mallet through
the hoops around the course.
As we stick the hoops into the
grass, I ask Aldeen if she's
going to Curtis's party.

"Yeah,"

she says, grabbing the blue mallet and ball.

"But scary movies are boring. I've seen a million of them."

I take the yellow ball and mallet and line up my first shot. I miss the hoop. Aldeen takes a shot and her ball smacks into mine.

"You didn't even aim for the hoop," I complain.

Her noogie-knuckle pops out.

"Tough bananas. Rocket shot!"

I hate this part of croquet.
Aldeen puts her blue ball
touching mine and holds it
down with her foot. Then she
winds up like Godzilla golfing
a home run and smacks it. Her
ball stays put. Mine zooms into
the prickle bush. "Your turn,"
says Aldeen.

By the time Aldeen's grandma comes, my ball has gone through a hoop once and in the prickle bush fourteen times. I have changed my mind about croquet.

Chapter Four

It Can't be that Bad . . .
Right?

At dinner I think about what Aldeen said. I've never seen a scary movie. If they're boring instead of scary, I don't have to worry. Maybe I should give one a try. If it's boring, cool. If it is scary, I can always ask

my parents to turn it off. I put
some broccoli on my fork to
show how good I am and go
for it.

"Can we watch a scary movie tonight?"

Dad looks surprised. He looks at Mom. Mom looks at me.

"Really?" she says.

"Remember what happened after the octopus movie?"

I remember. I watched this movie with my best friend Charlie.

Dad had to triple-check my room for two weeks. I was sure tentacles were oozing toward me in the dark.

"I'm way older now," I say. "And anyway that was squids, not octopuses," I say.

"*Octopi*," says Dad.

"Anything with no tentacles will be fine," I say.

"Pleeeeease?"

Mom smiles. "We'll see.
It could depend on whether
you're brave enough to eat
that broccoli."

I hate it when she does that.

As Mom and I load the dishwasher, Dad gets a movie ready. It's *The Wizard of Oz.* "But that's a baby movie," I complain,

"That's not scary."

Dad wiggles his eyebrows. "It has its moments."

He's right. I make it through the whole movie, but I'm glad Mom and Dad snuggle me between them.

Once, Mom asks if I want to
turn it off. I shake my head no.
I'm not sure what part it
is, because my eyes are shut
tight. After, I want my window
closed, to keep out flying
monkeys.

I'm even more scared about something else.

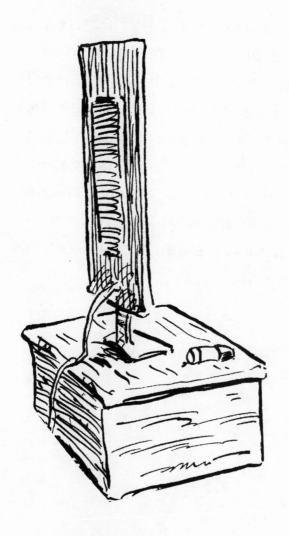

If *The Wizard of Oz* freaked me out, how am I going to make it through *Brain Eater*? Why can't I just be bored, like Aldeen? Maybe you don't get scared if everyone is scared of you. I'm not scary. If I chicken out in front of all my friends, I'll never sleep for the rest of my life.

Chapter Five

Revenge!

By lunch the next day I feel
better. That means I'm hungry
— until I see

Charlie has spaghetti.

Everybody's still talking
about what the *Brain Eater*

spaghetti is made of.

I reach into my own lunch bag — and pull out the biggest, ugliest spider I have ever seen. Charlie drops his fork.

"**AAAH!**" I yell and heave it away. The spider lands where Aldeen is arm wrestling Simon. They shriek and blast up like rockets.

For a second we're all stunned. Then someone starts laughing. It's Curtis. He walks over and picks up the spider. Its legs bobble like Aldeen's hair. He jiggles them at me.

"It's just a toy, Morgan."

Kids start laughing. Almost
everyone joins in. Even Charlie
snorts and grins. Aldeen
stands frozen, until Curtis
jiggles the spider again, right
in front of her face. She jumps
back, then stomps away. More
kids laugh.

"Payback, Morgan!"

Curtis calls. "Hey scaredy-cat,

meowwwwww!""

I take my cookies to eat outside. Aldeen is in the corner of the yard. "Get lost," she says.

"it wasn't my spider," I say,

"Curtis pranked me and I got, um . . . surprised. I didn't mean to scare you."

"*I wasn't scared,*" Aldeen hisses. She doesn't look at me. "I just don't like spiders. They're boring." Her hand snakes out and swipes a cookie. "Now get lost."

Chapter Six

Chilling
Tales

Aldeen comes to my place
again after school, Charlie too.

Nobody says
anything about
spiders.

We take snacks up to my
play fort. Charlie pulls a library
book out of his backpack:
Chilling Tales. The title is
written on a tombstone.

"Scary stories will be a good way to get ready for *Brain Eater*," Charlie says.

"Cool," I say. "I love scary books." I've never read a scary book, but it can't be as scary as a movie. At least, I hope not. Plus I don't want to look like a scaredy-cat again in front of Charlie and Aldeen.

I open *Chilling Tales* to the first story and start reading out loud. It's about a brother

and sister who get lost in a
cemetery at night. It sounds
pretty silly, so I do silly voices
for their talking bits. Then
the story gets a little scarier:
they find a just-dug-up grave
with an old, rotting coffin in
it. There's a scraping noise
coming from inside and a voice
is croaking,

"Help, help,"

and they get down in the grave, and right as the brother is about to open the coffin . . . Aldeen jumps up. "My grandma's here. I heard her car."

Charlie nods. His eyes are big. "Let's go check," he says, fast.

It sounds good to me. We all hurry to the driveway. Nobody's there.

"That story SUCKS,"
says Aldeen.

"It's too boring to finish.
Let's play croquet instead."
I don't even mind her rocket
shots.

After dinner, Dad and I go
to the mall to get Curtis a
birthday present.

We get him a croquet set
just like ours.

I'd rather get Curtis a giant
pterodactyl that would eat
his rubber spider and drop

him and *Brain Eater* on top of a mountain somewhere, but there's no pet store at the mall.

Chapter Seven

A Cunning
Plan

The night before the party,
Dad and I wrap the croquet
set. I get ribbon from the junk
drawer and find a pair of big
bug-eyed sunglasses in there,
too. They give me a totally

fantastic idea.

We finish wrapping,
then I ask if I can have the
sunglasses.

"All yours," he says,

"Mom said they make me
look like a space alien."

I wear the sunglasses up to the bathroom. In the mirror I see they do make you look like a space alien. Who cares? I grab Mom's earplugs for swimming and head back to the junk drawer to get a black marker.

I colour over the inside of the sunglass lenses with the marker and test my idea.

I turn on the TV, put on the glasses and stick the earplugs in. The picture turns to dim, flickering light, and the sound sinks to a murmur. It's perfect.

Now I can watch all the scary movies in the world and not be creeped out.

I feel for the remote and punch up the volume. I hear something about more ham.
I punch it up some more. Now "more ham" sounds more like "more hands."

I go to punch it up more and
the remote is yanked away. I
jump up and pop an earplug.
Music blares. The sunglasses
fall off. The TV screen blazes.

"MORGAN!"

somebody is yelling and
another voice booms, *"UP
NEXT AN ALL NEW—"*

Everything stops. In the silence Mom is staring at me, holding the remote. It's still pointed at the dead TV. "What on earth . . . ?" she says.

"Science experiment?"

I try.

"Hmm.

Well, you look like a mad scientist in those glasses.

C'mon, we're all playing croquet."

"I thought I looked like — never mind." We go play croquet. I'm so happy about my idea, I don't care what I look like.

Chapter Eight

Disaster!

It's party time and I'm ready.
I've got shades in one pocket
and earplugs in the other. I'll
look as bored as Aldeen through
Brain Eater. If anyone asks
about the glasses, I'll say
I just had eye surgery.

Curtis has a huge backyard.
There's a play fort twice as
big as mine, and a trampoline
and a basketball hoop. Curtis
tells everybody who can play
on what.

"No trampoline, Morgan. You might break it."

He runs off laughing. I wouldn't
go on the stupid trampoline
anyway. What might break
would be my shades.

Charlie is shooting baskets.
"Curtis says he lost *Brain
Eater*," he whispers, "But he
has something even better."
Charlie doesn't look too happy.
Nobody does. Behind him, I see
Aldeen slip into the house.

Curtis yells,
"Presents!"

Curtis rips through his gifts at warp speed. His mom reminds him to say thank you. There's a cool t-shirt from Charlie. Aldeen's present is *Chilling Tales*. It has the exact same scratch on the cover the library copy had. I look for Aldeen, but she's not around. Curtis opens the croquet set. He squints at it, frowning. "What the heck is this?" His mom nudges him. "I mean, thanks." He's already opening the next present.

Curtis's dad brings out hot dogs and hamburgers. We hustle to the picnic tables.

Suddenly Aldeen is back.

She tugs Lauren's hair. "Move over! You too, tubbo."

She squishes in and
something pokes my leg hard.

Crunch.

Uh oh. I feel my pocket.
My shades are snapped in two.

Noooo.

I still have the earplugs. I can sit near the back and look at the floor.

I dig out my earplugs to make sure. Curtis's dad leans in with more burgers. He bumps my elbow. An earplug flies into Mark's pop. He picks it up and drinks. A funny look comes over his face. "I think I just swallowed a bug," he says slowly.

"**Ewwwwwww**,"

everybody says, except me. I don't say anything at all.

Chapter Nine

Desperate Measures

What now? I'm doomed. I'm so scared I can't even eat.

But wait a sec. No movie till we finish eating, right? What if I can eat? It's my only chance. Luckily, I'm good at eating.

I grab a burger and wonder
what time Mom will pick me up.
Beside me, Aldeen snaps,

"Where's the bathroom?"

Something hard smacks me
again as she shoves back up.
I don't care. I'm piling chips
and hot dogs onto my plate.
Then I eat, as slowly as I can.
I count every chew. Kids are
finishing, I'm still munching.
Is everyone done? I take
some more.

"Cake time!" Curtis calls.

"Ibe mwot dub," I call,
around some hot dog.

"Well, hurry up," snaps
Aldeen. She's back. What does
she care? She's not scared by
scary movies. Still, I'm getting
full. I swallow the hot dog.
I can stall over cake, too.

We do the singing and the
candles and making a wish.
It takes a long time to serve
everybody.

Excellent.

I ask for seconds, even
though I'm really full. I ask for
thirds. Mom must be coming

soon. Charlie stares at me. I'm
chewing in slow motion. I'm so
stuffed I can hardly swallow.
I put my fork down. I've stalled
as long as I can. Mom's not
here. Curtis says,

"Movie time!"

We all troop down to the
basement. I walk slowly. Every
step makes my stomach lurch.
I feel as if I've swallowed a
basketball. It's okay, though.
Nobody but Curtis goes any

faster. Everyone looks as
uncomfortable as I feel.

Downstairs there's popcorn,
but I don't want to look at it.

"It's *Super Kidz 3*," Curtis's
dad says. Behind him, Curtis
grins and holds up a different
movie case.

"Where are the remotes?" asks Curtis's dad. "This won't turn on."

Curtis's mom comes in with them.

"Why were these in the bathroom?"

she asks.

The bathroom? I look at Aldeen. She stares at the ceiling.

The batteries are missing. They get more. Still nothing works. Aldeen stares at the wall. "Everything's been disconnected," says Curtis's dad. "Curtis, what have you been up to?"

"I didn't do anything,"

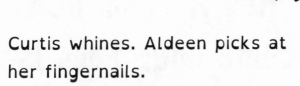

Curtis whines. Aldeen picks at her fingernails.

Everything gets plugged back in. "Whew. I'll get you started," says Curtis's dad. The room goes quiet. As soon as he leaves, we all know Curtis is going to switch movies. I try to swallow. No one is smiling. Kaely and Ben might cry. Behind her witchy hair Aldeen's face has gone pale as vanilla icing. The room is cool but I feel sweaty. Charlie turns to me. His face changes too: his eyebrows bunch up, and he says,

"Hey Morgan, how come your face is so white?"

Before I can tell him, I throw up.

Chapter Ten

Escape!

Everyone yells and scrambles
out of the way. I would too if
I wasn't barfing. Curtis's mom
calls,

"Backyard, kids!"

Nobody moves slowly now.

"Way to wreck it, Morgan,"

says Curtis.

"It's okay, Morgan," says Curtis's dad.

"Nobody plans to be sick, Curtis. You go outside too."

He takes me to the washroom and helps clean me up, then gets me a glass of water. When I finally go out I'm wearing the t-shirt Charlie gave Curtis. It fits, kind of.

A soccer game has started. Nobody races over to high-five me or say, "Way to go!" But kids ask if I'm feeling better. It's easy to see they are feeling better, even Curtis. Charlie says,

"Let's play croquet."

We open the box and set up the hoops. Charlie says, "I saw the other movie Curtis had. It was *The Wizard of Oz*. Have you seen it? The flying monkeys and grabby trees creep me out."

"Me too," I say.

Charlie takes red to go first. Aldeen shoves the green mallet at me. I step out of noogie range and take a chance:

"What did you do with the batteries?"

Aldeen stares at me, then her eyes flick left, then right. "They took three flushes," she mutters. Her eyes squinch up. "I just didn't want to be bored."

"Right," I say.

Aldeen says, "Can you barf like that anytime you want to?"

"I could probably do it again," I say. What I'm thinking

is, I am *so* never doing that
again.

Aldeen nods.

"Cool," she says, then,

"Rocket shot!"

She blasts my ball across
the yard.

More titles in

Be Brave, MORGAN!

Daredevil Morgan

Be Brave, Morgan!

Daredevil Morgan

Ted Staunton/Illustrated by Bill Slavin

Morgan's best friend Charlie urges him to try the GraviTwirl ride at the Fall Fair. But Morgan is focused on his homegrown contender for the Perfect Pumpkin contest. That is, until Aldeen Hummel, the Godzilla of Grade Three, drops it!

Morgan faces Aldeen in a bumper car War. Aldeen dares him to go on the Asteroid Belt ride. Will Morgan be brave enough to try? And can he still win the Best Pumpkin Pie contest with the remains of his squished squash?

Morgan on Ice

Morgan doesn't like to skate, and he's determined not to learn. What he really wants to do is go see Monster Truck-A-Rama with Charlie. Aldeen is not impressed since Morgan already agreed to go to Princesses on Ice with her. Can Morgan keep everyone happy, or is he skating on thin ice?

Morgan's Got Game

Be Brave, Morgan!

Morgan's Got Game

Ted Staunton/Illustrated by Bill Slavin

Morgan is left out of the loop when everyone at school begins bringing their Robogamer Z7 to school, linking up online with one another, and playing at recess and lunch. Charlie lets Morgan use his Z7 every now and then, but clearly you're not cool unless you have one of your own.

Poor Morgan is reduced to playing other games with Aldeen for something to do. Finally his parents relent, but Morgan learns that sometimes gaming is more trouble than it's worth!